William A.
1994-

D0175045

Esther Hautzig

RICHES

illustrated by Donna Diamond

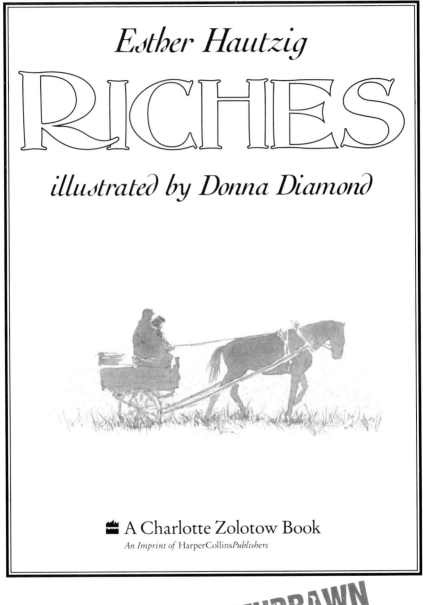

A Charlotte Zolotow Book
An Imprint of HarperCollins*Publishers*

RICHES

Text copyright © 1992 by Esther Hautzig
Illustrations copyright © 1992 by Donna Diamond
Printed in the U.S.A. All rights reserved.
1   2   3   4   5   6   7   8   9   10
First Edition

Library of Congress Cataloging-in-Publication Data
Hautzig, Esther Rudomin.
  Riches / Esther Hautzig ; illustrated by Donna Diamond.
     p.   cm.
  "A Charlotte Zolotow book."
  Summary: After following the advice of the wisest rabbi in the
area, a rich storekeeper discovers that giving of himself is better
than merely giving money.
  ISBN 0-06-022259-X. — ISBN 0-06-022260-3 (lib. bdg.)
  [1. Conduct of life—Fiction.   2. Money—Fiction.   3. Jews—
Fiction.]   I. Diamond, Donna, ill.   II. Title.
PZ7.H289Ri   1992   89-26904
[Fic]—dc20   CIP
                                                              AC

With rich memories
of Victor Chapin
and John Schaffner

ESTHER HAUTZIG

For my mother and father with love

DONNA DIAMOND

A long time ago a couple named Samuel and Chaya-Rivka lived in Antokol, a small town on the river Vilia. They were married for many, many years. Samuel and Chaya-Rivka raised two fine sons and a good daughter and they worked very hard side by side all their lives.

When Samuel and Chaya-Rivka reached three score and ten years of age they were considered a rich old couple. Their dry goods store was considered the best in their little corner of Eastern Europe. Samuel sold the best scythes, hoes, hammers, saws, axes and nails. Farmers, merchants and builders trusted him and came from all over the area to buy tools and farm implements from Samuel.

"Always buy the best you can and it will last you a lifetime," Samuel told his customers. And they did.

Chaya-Rivka stocked the prettiest fabrics, yarns and trimmings on the shelves of their store. Women from towns and villages near and far came to buy materials and buttons, threads and needles. Chaya-Rivka was always jolly and friendly and she did not stint a few extra centimeters when she measured out the goods.

She even gave an extra button to everyone who bought a dozen. "A baker's

dozen," she'd say, smiling, "even though you can't eat them!"

And they were always generous with their money. They gave food and clothing to the orphanage. They sent money to the old-age home in Antokol. They dropped silver coins into the cups of all the beggars on the street and those who came to their store.

But Samuel and Chaya-Rivka never had time to stop and visit at the orphanage or at the old-age home. They were too busy to speak to the beggars on the street or in the store. All Samuel and Chaya-Rivka had time for was work and more work.

TWO

One evening, as they were tidying up the store, Samuel said to Chaya-Rivka, "Maybe it is time we stopped working? Soon it will be fifty years that we are married and have opened our store. Shouldn't there be more to life than hard work?"

"I would like to stay home and read holy books in peace and think about what I read without the bustle of the store."

Chaya-Rivka sighed as she rolled up the large bolts of fabric and put them on the shelf. "But hard work is most pleasing to the Almighty," she quietly added as she put the spools of thread into the glass case under the counter.

"Maybe you are right, dear wife. Hard work is pleasing to the Almighty. And I don't know what useful deed we can perform when we no longer work! Admire nature? Look at stars? I have no answers!"

Samuel pulled on his mustache and

looked away from Chaya-Rivka.

"I think I shall consult with the Gaon of Vilna, the wisest rabbi of all. I will go to him and seek his advice."

Chaya-Rivka was astonished. The Gaon of Vilna was the most revered of all rabbis in their region. Everyone respected him and followed his teachings. But she'd heard that the Gaon did not speak to strangers. He prayed and studied almost round the clock. People said he slept for only two hours out of every twenty-four. In half-hour periods! In an unheated room! And Samuel would go to seek the revered Gaon's advice on what he and she should do when they stopped working?

"Go to Vilna and see him," she nevertheless told Samuel. "Perhaps no matter is too small if it's done to please God as well as man."

THREE

Samuel came to the house of the Gaon of Vilna just before dusk. As always, he put on his prayer shawl to recite his prayers. When the prayers were over, Samuel remained in the shadows of the room and waited for the Gaon to take a respite from his studies. Finally the Gaon turned his head. Samuel quickly approached him.

"Rabbi, I am a stranger to you and yet I've come to ask you for a great favor."

The Gaon smiled. "Amongst us there are no strangers. Sit down, dear friend." He pointed to a chair and lit another candle on his table. "Do you have a place to spend the night? Do you need food or clothing?"

"No, Rabbi, I lack for nothing. I have a fine wife, good children, a comfortable home. We have a good business as well in Antokol."

"Why then did you come to me?" asked the Gaon.

"I need your counsel!" Samuel cried out. "My wife and I have worked hard all our lives. Now that we are old we want to stop. But what should we *do* that will be pleasing to the Almighty when we no longer work?"

The Gaon did not seem annoyed or surprised. He stroked his beard in silence and observed Samuel. At last he spoke.

"I think you should become a horse-and-cart driver in Antokol."

Samuel leaned across the table in astonishment. "It would be pleasing to the Almighty that I do the simplest work in our town? I don't need the money! I can't take away business from Jeremiah, who drives the horse and cart in Antokol!"

"You won't do it to earn money," the Gaon firmly replied. "Take your horse and cart onto deserted roads outside Antokol. Do not seek business in town."

"And my wife? What can she do? She says she'd like to stay at home and study prayer books in peace."

"Good," the Gaon replied. "Then she should stay home and study. Far better that she should use her mind on books than on idle chatter."

Samuel and the Gaon looked intently at each other. At last Samuel got up.

"If you believe that this is what we should do, then we shall do it, for you are the wisest rabbi in all the world!"

"There is no one wisest rabbi in the world! Everyone is a little wise and a little foolish. Sometimes more, sometimes less."

The Gaon reached for his books and moved the candles closer.

"Come back after you've driven your horse and cart for three months, except on Sabbath of course! I want to know how you've fared."

Samuel returned to Antokol and told Chaya-Rivka of the Gaon's advice. She too was astonished.

"After all the years you've spent as a busy and successful storekeeper, after all of that you should become a simple horse-and-cart driver?"

Since Chaya-Rivka was not only a smart and industrious woman but a pious one as well, she did not argue very long

with the Gaon's edict. And she was pleased that the Gaon had told Samuel that she could stay at home and study books.

Perhaps by studying the books I'll learn about wise rabbis' teachings and understand their advice, she thought.

15

Samuel and Chaya-Rivka spent the entire summer showing their children and grandchildren how to run the store so their customers would remain happy. They checked their stock. They paid their bills and collected what was owed them. Everything was set in order.

FIVE

When all the holidays—Rosh Hashanah, Yom Kippur and Succoth—were over, Samuel bought a horse and cart. From that day on Samuel and his light-brown mare bumped along deserted, rutted roads outside Antokol.

Sometimes Samuel glimpsed farmers digging up the last of their summer gardens. Other days he saw nothing but

trees in the red-and-golden glory of fall colors. Sometimes he stopped his cart and just looked across the fields, up into the sky at birds in flight, at forests. In years past he had seen these same trees but had no time to stop. He had had no time to admire nature.

When he came home, Chaya-Rivka would often eagerly inquire: "What happened today?"

"Nothing happened," Samuel would reply slowly. "But there was a birch tree with leaves that were bright yellow against its white bark. It shone like a beam of sunlight, even though the day was cloudy."

Chaya-Rivka was surprised. Never did Samuel tell her how a birch tree looked, and he'd seen them all his life!

SIX

When the weather became chilly and windy, Chaya-Rivka asked with great concern, "Couldn't you stay at home on this cold and blustery day?"

"No," Samuel replied. "The Gaon said that I should drive out every day, except on Sabbath of course, for three months. And so I shall."

Chaya-Rivka knew that it was useless to argue with her husband. She gave him an extra-warm sweater to wear beneath

his coat. She wound a large and soft scarf around his neck.

"Come back early if you get chilled. Hot broth and tea are always ready for you here at home!"

"Stop fussing over me, dear wife," Samuel said with a big smile.

"I'm not fussing, Samuel! I am taking care of you, as I said I would when we were married nearly fifty years ago!" Chaya-Rivka's eyes sparkled. "God be with you today and always," she called out as he drove away.

The countryside was deserted as Samuel drove up and down the roads outside Antokol. The trees were nearly bare, the wind blew strongly. Suddenly he noticed a small figure on the horizon.

"Giddyup," he called gently to his mare. The horse broke into a trot. When Samuel came closer, he found that it was

an old woman, bent under a heavy sack slung on her back.

"Peace to you, my friend," he called out. "Your load looks heavy. What's in it?" The woman put down her heavy sack. Samuel saw that she was crippled and frail.

"I've been to the potato fields around here. I've dug up potatoes that farmers left behind, buried deep inside the earth. They're in my sack." She pointed to it with pride.

Samuel frowned. The potatoes farmers left in the ground were always small, half frozen and spoiled.

Perhaps I should give her a few rubles to buy good potatoes?

Something stopped him.

She is not a beggar and does not ask for anything of me. And she looks pleased with her findings.

"Would you like me to drive you home in my cart?" he asked.

"Oh, yes, I would," the old woman replied. "But unless you are the Prophet Elijah in disguise I cannot go with you! Ordinary cart drivers must be paid for their trouble, and I haven't a kopeck on me."

She bent down to lift her sack.

"Well, I'm not the Prophet Elijah," Samuel said with a smile, "but tell me where you live."

"I live near Lubtch, with two cats I found in the alley," she replied, "about two kilometers from here."

"I'm on my way to Lubtch right now," Samuel quickly said, "and since I'm going there anyway, I'll be glad to have you ride with me."

"Well, if you are going that way, I will ride with you. Even if you're not Elijah!"

She flung the sack into the cart and climbed in. Samuel clicked his tongue and the cart lurched along the bumpy road.

The woman hummed a song about Elijah, a song every child and grown-up knew, and looked slyly at Samuel. Samuel hummed companionably and smiled until they reached her hut outside of Lubtch.

"Oh, thank you, thank you," the woman said with a big smile. "Now I'm not a bit tired. I can roast potatoes for my cats and me, and we'll have a fine meal tonight."

She looked so happy and proud that Samuel was glad he did not offer her money. He felt glad about what he'd done for her instead.

As he rode back to Antokol, Samuel thought how nice it would be to tell his Chaya-Rivka that someone thought he was the Prophet Elijah doing good deeds in disguise! Just like in the books she was reading every day.

SEVEN

Soon snow covered the ground. The air was bitter cold and winds blew ever harder all day long. Still Samuel drove out each morning, after prayers, into the countryside, just as the Gaon had told him to do. The three months weren't over and Samuel was determined to keep his promise.

Just as he left Antokol one day, he noticed a young boy carrying a baby in his arms, walking slowly down the road.

He wore a threadbare jacket. The baby
was wrapped in a flimsy blanket.

"Where are you going, my child?"
Samuel called out.

"To Volokumpia, to find my family," he
answered hesitantly. "My brother is ill
and getting worse."

"But Volokumpia is far away! You
cannot walk there! And carrying a sick
baby! Where are your parents?"

"They are both dead," the boy

whispered, and began to weep. "Father died last spring. We came a short while ago to Antokol, so my mother could find work. Then she got ill and died also. We have no family here and I want to go to Volokumpia to find my aunt and uncle. They will help us!" Large tears rolled down the boy's cheeks.

"I'm going to Volokumpia on business, my child," Samuel quickly said. "I'll take you there and we'll find your relatives."

He got down and helped the young boy and his baby brother climb into the cart. Samuel covered them with straw and hay, and he wound his warm scarf around the baby.

"Are you a Lamed-Vovnik?" the young boy whispered to Samuel. "Can you be one of the thirty-six just men who live under humble guises and perform good deeds?"

Samuel patted the children with a happy smile. The mare took off as soon as Samuel tugged the reins and they sped along to Volokumpia.

Samuel did not return home till very late that night. His eyelashes and mustache had turned white with frost. His hands and feet were numb from the icy wind. Chaya-Rivka was beside herself with worry when she met him at the door.

"What happened to you, dear husband?" she cried out.

"I helped two orphans find their aunt and uncle all the way in Volokumpia." Samuel patted Chaya-Rivka's shoulder. "The older one asked me if I was a Lamed-Vovnik," he added shyly.

"Who knows? I've read a lot about them lately and maybe you are!" Chaya-Rivka answered proudly.

EIGHT

Only two weeks were left before Samuel was to go back to Vilna to see the Gaon. Although the roads were covered with snow and the weather cruel, he still went out each morning with his horse and cart.

One Friday afternoon, while the snow glistened in the sun, Samuel met Gabriel, the beggar, who sang each day on Antokol streets and in the marketplace. Samuel often dropped coins into his tin cup, but he never had time to stop and talk, or comment on his songs.

Gabriel trudged along the road, feeling his way with his stick, for he was nearly blind.

"Peace to you, my friend," Samuel called out.

"And to you," replied Gabriel, squinting into Samuel's direction. "Who may you be?"

"Oh, just a horse-and-cart driver, going home for Sabbath. And where are you going?"

"I'm going home to Nemenchin for Sabbath, too, but I'm afraid I won't get there before sundown. My eyesight is getting worse. I misjudged the time of day."

The beggar looked in the direction of the setting sun.

Samuel got off his cart. He put his hands on Gabriel's shoulders.

"You'll never get to Nemenchin on time for Sabbath. Come home with me, my friend. We'll welcome Sabbath together."

Gabriel peered into Samuel's face.

"You look like Samuel, the rich storekeeper. But it cannot be; rich storekeepers don't ask beggars to their homes for Sabbath."

Samuel did not reply. He helped Gabriel get into his cart. When Samuel and Gabriel arrived home, Chaya-Rivka was already waiting at the door. She looked at Samuel and then at Gabriel.

"I've brought an honored guest for Sabbath," Samuel quickly said. He helped Gabriel inside the room, where the table was set and candles were lit. The house was filled with all the good smells of Sabbath cooking.

"What is your name, dear host?" the beggar asked. "Your house is warm and it smells of foods cooked by rich folk."

"My name is Samuel, and my wife's is Chaya-Rivka."

"So you are the rich shopkeeper after all," the beggar cried out.

"What of it? I'm just a man, like you!" Samuel answered with spirit.

They had a good Sabbath eve together. They enjoyed the food, sang hymns and talked of things they knew.

"You must come to welcome the Sabbath with us each Friday and stay the night. We have room for you and a soft bed with down blankets. Tomorrow we'll go to synagogue together and say the Havdallah prayers here as well," Samuel told Gabriel.

"Yes, yes," Chaya-Rivka said. Gabriel happily accepted.

NINE

The three months were over. It was time for Samuel to see the Gaon of Vilna.

Again Samuel waited a long time in the shadows of the Gaon's synagogue. When at last Samuel faced the Gaon, the rabbi quietly asked:

"Well, Samuel, how did matters go with your wife? Did she read and study much?"

"Oh, yes, Gaon, she did. She has read legends about Elijah the Prophet, and

stories of the Lamed-Vovniks. She has knowledge she has never had before."

"That is good, and pleasing to the Almighty. And what did you accomplish?" the Gaon continued gently.

"Not much, I fear to say."

"Really?" the Gaon persisted. "Tell me what you saw."

Samuel recounted his trips on deserted roads. He described the beauty of nature, the changing seasons, cloud formations, falling snow and fields glistening in the sun.

"I never did have time to see God's

world in all its beauty before. But was that enough to please the Almighty?" Samuel peered anxiously into the Gaon's face.

"Seeing, really *seeing*, Samuel! That is pleasing to the Creator of the Universe. How many people do that in a lifetime?" The Gaon looked kindly at Samuel.

"And now tell me what you did," he continued.

"I took a crippled woman to her home in my horse and cart. She carried a heavy sack with potatoes she had dug up after the farmers finished their harvest." Samuel's face was creased with worry. "Maybe you know how bitter to the taste such potatoes are? But she looked so happy that she had found them! Should I have given her money to buy good potatoes instead?"

"Tell me more," the Gaon said, without answering Samuel's question.

"Well, I drove young orphans to Volokumpia to find their family." Samuel lowered his eyes. "Would it have been wiser and better in God's eyes had I given them money to ride the stagecoach?"

Samuel pulled nervously on his mustache before he went on speaking.

"And I asked Gabriel the beggar to my home when he was going to be late getting home for Sabbath one cold Friday afternoon, and I also asked him to spend every Sabbath with us for the rest of our days."

The Gaon sat very still and observed Samuel with great kindness.

"Tell me, Rabbi, should I have given Gabriel a generous donation instead, so he would not need to sing on the streets of Antokol and wait for coins to be put in his cup?"

"Samuel, my friend, you did right in all

three cases. To give of *yourself* and not of your money is God's special way of bestowing riches on the giver and the receiver."

The Gaon put his hands on Samuel's head.

"Go home to your dear wife. Pray each day, as always. Give charity, as ever. But also give of *yourself* whenever and wherever you can."

And Samuel went home a happy man. He told Chaya-Rivka what the Gaon had said. She was proud and happy, too.

For Samuel and Chaya-Rivka's fiftieth wedding anniversary, soon after the holiday of Passover, when all the spring planting was completed, their children and grandchildren and people from the entire area came to celebrate. The old

woman came bearing a delicious potato
kugel. The young orphans came with
their aunt and uncle, carrying a bouquet
of flowers from the fields around Antokol. And Gabriel came too and sang a
special song in honor of the celebration.